Shakes Here

Kim Wedler

TSL Drama

First published in Great Britain in 2022
By TSL Publications, Rickmansworth

Copyright © 2022 Kim Wedler

ISBN: 978-1-914245-63-3

Cover courtesy of : Kim Wedler

Cast

Victor Abbey – 50 years old; wearing a crisp white shirt with the "Shakes Here" logo and matching white trousers.

Sally Abbey – 40s, dressed in the Shakes Here uniform.

Leigh Abbey – 18, dressed in the Shakes Here uniform.

Flo Cottleworth – early 60s; wearing a floral shell suit, with a bum bag. Has a very broad Liverpudlian accent.

Patricia Trout – 60s; dressed in a leopard skin top, black tight skirt, clutch bag and has an enormous beehive hairstyle. She has a phony Joanna Lumley type voice.

Bovey Tracey – 50s; his straw hat is elegantly tilted. He is dressed in an expensive shirt, top button undone, beige linen slacks and canvas shoes.

Byron Bay – 20s; blond and bronzed. He is dressed in beach wear.

Running Time
approx 45 mins

Scene 1

The curtains are opened to the tune of "Oh I do like to be beside the seaside".

The setting is an ice cream parlour. Seagulls are heard.

VICTOR   [*holding a milkshake in his hand, enters singing*] "Oh I do like to be beside the seaside".

VICTOR: Bit of music, I think! Another wonderful creation! [*sips the milkshake*] Delicious! [*puts it on the counter, and moves glasses around*]

Another, wonderful Summer!! [*looks at his watch*] 9:45! 15 minutes and the swish of the open sign and the delightful sound of the welcoming bell, as "Shakes Here" ice cream parlour is open for business!

The doorbell is sounded, and Flo Cottleworth enters.

VICTOR: Oh, I'm sorry madam, we're not actually open for [*looks at his watch again*] 9:48, 12 minutes.

FLO: Oh, I just wondered if …

VICTOR: Oh, what the hell, let's live dangerously. So, my wife and I have owned this establishment for five years now. We live in a wonderful cottage up on the hill, called St

Michaels. With our daughter Leigh, who also helps in our parlour. Although between you and me, she's on a gap year until she goes to university. But I must say, I wouldn't mind her just working here, obviously moving up to a management position and then, when myself and my wife retire, she could take it over. I know, I should say education is important, but there is something to be said for the university of life. Obviously, it incorporates maths skills, people skills and good old-fashioned hard work.

FLO: Is it …

VICTOR: Is it wise to give up a degree in Parapsychology?

FLO: I don't …

VICTOR: I didn't know either. It's the study of the paranormal. Yes, the course actually exists! Unless she wants to be a "Ghost Buster" which is highly unlikely, it's a waste of time.

FLO: I think …

VICTOR: I think she just wants to go for the boys!! Derived from liggin'–

FLO: What …

VICTOR: Wasting time lying around with no real purpose. It's a Yorkshire saying. Why do we have northern accents I hear you ask? Because we're Northern. Well, we're actually from Mossy Bottom, South Yorkshire. Left it all behind for idyllic Torquay.

FLO: Could you tell me …?

VICTOR: What our secret is to be running a successful ice cream parlour? It's our people skills and our ability to listen to what our customers want!

FLO: Well, really, I'd just like to …

VICTOR: Have a seat and look at the menu …?

FLO: No, I…

VICTOR: ...Know what you want. That's the customers prerogative. Well, you won't be disappointed I can assure you!! This season we have introduced two new flavours "Macdeath by chocolate" and "Mid-summer nights cream" both absolutely delightful. But if you have something else in mind. I would like to say the "Baileys banger" is a delectable mix of coffee ice cream for the base, with Baileys and Kahlua; and Irish cream and a splash of milk to add creaminess. You can also choose either vanilla or chocolate ice cream instead if you like. It is our over 18 milkshake, so ... I hope you've brought ID young lady. [*winks and snorts*]

FLO: I just came in ...

VICTOR: I know, and we're happy to have you!

FLO: I just came in to ask, where the post box is actually.

VICTOR: Oh, I see, there's one on the corner of the street next to rocks away, rock shop.

FLO: Lovely, thanks. I must say this is really nice in here. I'm Flo by the way! Yes, I will come back with me bezzie, Patricia. We're staying in the bed and breakfast above the chippie. She's having her hair done at the moment, she only had it done yesterday on the way down here. She got up this morning, she opened the window and said she could smell the fish frying, and the smell of salt and vinegar in the air. I hardly smelt it, but she said it had ruined her hair. So off she's gone. I hope the hair-dresser doesn't put the blow dryer on, she's had that many facelifts she'll probably melt.

VICTOR: I detect a Liverpool accent!

FLO: G'wed lad! Scouser through and through, so is Pat. You wouldn't think it. After she got divorced from her third husband she put on this phoney accent, silly mare.

VICTOR: Three husbands!!

FLO: Four actually. The last one left her for his secretary!

VICTOR: Bit cliché!

FLO:	That's what we thought, until we found out his name was Brian and he drove a forklift! That's when I told her to jib him off and come down here with me. I love the seaside, dipping me toes in. Patricia won't in case she gets her hair wet. There's that much lacquer in it, she'd probably come out looking like pebble dashing. Can't dip your toes in the Mersey, that's for sure!
VICTOR:	Most likely have to have shots!
FLO:	Oh, we always go to the pub after, yes!
VICTOR:	No, I meant … Oh never mind. I went to Liverpool Tech, culinary skills!
FLO:	'll see you later, turrah! [*she leaves, the bell on the door sounds and the door shuts*]
VICTOR:	My goodness! She can talk! Check my list [*removes a pad and pencil from his pocket*] Glasses, check, tablecloths check, menus, check, spoons … a few.
	The doorbell is sounded, and LEIGH ABBEY *enters. The sound of texting is heard.*
VICTOR:	Oh, Leigh about time, did you? …
LEIGH:	Just a second dad. [*text sound stops, a bleep is heard.* LEIGH *laughs*] Oh, how funny!! [*text sound is heard, stops, a bleep is heard.* LEIGH *laughs*]
VICTOR:	Leigh?
LEIGH:	Dad? [*pause*] Sorry, I just met Byron. He's the new owner of the "Surfs away" shop, at the harbour, we got talking.
VICTOR:	And you gave him your number?
LEIGH:	Yes, well he just wanted to check I got home safely!
VICTOR:	From the harbour? If I look out the window, I can see the harbour. What did he think, you were going to fall into the sea?
LEIGH:	Oh, Dad! [*pause*] Guess what? He must have seen me around; he knew I worked here. He'd even found out my name.

VICTOR: So not because you had your uniform on, which says it and your name badge. Also, the high street is not near the discount shop which is where I told you to go. Did you get the spoons?

LEIGH: Erm, they didn't have any way.

VICTOR: "Spoons r Us", with the slogan "a spoon for your every need!" didn't have any spoons?!

LEIGH: Alright, I'll go again.

VICTOR: Maybe text your mum, she went down to give out leaflets!

The doorbell is sounded, and SALLY ABBEY *enters. The sound of texting is heard.*

VICTOR: Oh, Sally would you mind? ...

SALLY: Just a second love. [*text sound stops, a bleep is heard.* SALLY *laughs*] Oh, how funny!! [*text sound is heard, stops, a bleep is heard.* SALLY *laughs*]

VICTOR: Sally?

SALLY: Victor? [*pause*] Sorry, I have just been talking to a lovely young man called Byron. He's the new owner of the "Surfs away" shop, at the harbour, we got talking.

VICTOR: And you gave him your number?

SALLY: Yes, well he just wanted to check I got home safely!

VICTOR: From the harbour? Did he give you a life jacket just in case?

SALLY: Sorry! [*pause*] Oh, he was quite charming. He must have seen me around; he knew I worked here. He'd even found out my name.

VICTOR: The apple doesn't fall far from the tree! Spoons Sally, spoons!!

SALLY: Yes Victor?

VICTOR: We need spoons. We haven't got any.

SALLY: Victor, there is a large box, on the floor next to the counter. What does it say on it?

VICTOR:	This way up.
SALLY:	On the label.
VICTOR:	[*pause*] Oh yes, spoons my love.
SALLY:	Yes! Why don't you put them out back with the serviettes?
VICTOR:	Which are next to …?
SALLY:	Oh, for goodness' sake. I'll come with you! Leigh mind the shop. We won't be long!
VICTOR:	Don't forget, greet the customer with a smile, not a nod of the head as you continue to look at your phone.
LEIGH:	[*nods head*] Mm hmm.
VICTOR:	Leigh, put your phone away!
LEIGH:	Ok! What's that on the counter?
VICTOR:	My latest creation. "As you like it".
LEIGH:	You don't know how I like it.
VICTOR:	No, that's what it's called, try it!
LEIGH:	Maybe in a minute.
	VICTOR *and* SALLY *exit.*
	The doorbell is sounded, and BOVEY TRACEY *enters.*
LEIGH:	Good morning sir, welcome to Shakes Here, can I see you to your table?
BOVEY:	Good morning young lady, you most certainly can. [*breathes in deeply*] Oh the wonderful sea air! Its rhythmical ebb and flow. Its potential for cleansing and, if I may quote Shakespeare "its reflection for the order of the universe".
LEIGH:	Erm, Ok.
BOVEY:	I would like a table, not near the front as it can get a little distracting, with the sound of your charming little bell. Probably at the back, but not too near the kitchen, the clattering of glasses can be quite tiresome. Maybe not the middle of the establishment as it's a walk

through to the lavatory, the payment area and if I'm right in thinking ... can be an area for the congregation of young mothers and their offspring. They can be rather noisy, sticky, and rather pungent.

LEIGH: Well, I ...

BOVEY: Oh, here is fine. Yes, I sat here last year! In the delightful alcove.

LEIGH: Oh, you mean the small table, under the stairs? Yes, that's fine. There is no one here at the moment, so I think you'll be fine! I will bring you a menu.

BOVEY: Last year I was served by a delightful creature, she created me the most exquisite blend! [*pause*] Oh yes! I shan't forget. [*pause*] Exotic, like a pure ray of sunshine. More beautiful than a summer's day!

LEIGH: Can you remember what the milkshake was called?

BOVEY: I meant the delightful waitress!

LEIGH: Oh, I'm not sure ...

BOVEY: A complexion of cream, an essence of Lilly ...

LEIGH: We don't have a server called Lilly.

BOVEY: No, the essence of Lilly of the Valley. She made this milkshake with love.

LEIGH: I ...

BOVEY: Titania!

LEIGH: We definitely don't have a Titania!

BOVEY: That is what she called her creation, Titania Banana! A luxuriously thick, smooth ice cream flecked with bourbon vanilla pods which gave it an intensely deep vanilla taste. It smelt fresh and had a rich intense flavour. Its creaminess was likened to clotted cream and a pleasant nutty undertone. The thinly sliced bananas added a strong sweetness.

LEIGH: Are you a food critic?

BOVEY: Oh goodness no, I am a ...

VICTOR and SALLY return

SALLY: I told you! If you put everything in alphabetical order you won't lose anything!

A is for the avocados. B bananas, C cinnamon, and so on …

VICTOR: Listen, if I'm creating, I don't have time to put it all back in alphabetical order. What was 'I' for again?

SALLY: Idiot, maybe.

BOVEY: Oh, Sienna!

SALLY: Erm, it's Sally!

BOVEY: Oh, a thousand apologies!

SALLY: Bovey Tracey!! [*silly girly laugh*] How are you?

BOVEY: All the better for seeing you! My pulchritudinous brunette!

LEIGH: So, you were describing my mum!! Gross!

BOVEY: Now my darling. What was that milkshake you made me?

SALLY: Please take a seat. I will bring you a menu.

BOVEY sits, SALLY gets a menu.

BOVEY: Oh, I cannot see it on the menu!

SALLY: Look on the first column, fifth one down.

BOVEY: [*reads*] Oh, well isn't that something! I am almost close to tears! You renamed it! The Banana Bovey! A great honour! May I ask, why the change? Taking *my* name, that of a mere, humble mystery writer to decorate your milkshake, rather than that of "Titania" – which means Land of Giants and is of Greek origin. An iconic character from the works of Shakespeare's *Midsummer Night's Dream*?

SALLY: Well, after you left last summer, it wasn't quite as popular.

VICTOR: Oh, I remember now. It took on a bit of an adult theme.

BOVEY: Oh, the locals not keen on a good bourbon. Too high brow for them.

SALLY: No, it was the name of the milkshake, instead of Titania Banana ... It became. Booby banana, show us your Titania's, Busty banana ... Show us your bananaramas ... Titty booboo, is that a banana in your pocket or are ...

BOVEY: You needn't continue! I understand! Mere peasants!

SALLY: Of course, erm what are you working on this time Bovey? I love your books!

BOVEY: So, kind of you to say, Stephanie.

SALLY: Sally.

BOVEY: It's another mystery of course, my fifth in the series of "English Riviera Mysteries". This one focuses in a country village. The residents are in the process of setting up the village fete. One of the most popular activities is that of the muffin competition. The locals all make their mouth-watering, original muffins to be judged for a competition.

SALLY: Oh yes.

BOVEY: Well, just before the prestigious event, one of the competitors is found dead!

SALLY: Oh, my goodness.

BOVEY: Yes! It will have you on the edge of your seat.

SALLY: I don't doubt that at all. *I love you Moore* was fantastic. We even read it for my book club. The ladies loved it!

BOVEY: Oh, such high praise. This one is due to be released this September. I will send you a copy. I insist.

SALLY: Oh, that would be wonderful! Now let me go and create your milkshake! Victor, a word please.

VICTOR *and* SALLY *move behind the counter.*

SALLY: [*whispers*] Victor, go out the back and get a bottle of good quality bourbon.

VICTOR: We've got some on the top shelf in the kitchen.

SALLY:	I said *good quality Bourbon*. The stuff we've already got is Ok for the locals, but not for our superior guest. Believe *me* he *will* know!
VICTOR:	Alright! But don't blame me if we get busy.
SALLY:	Leigh, can wait on tables.
VICTOR:	Yes, let's hope she can!

VICTOR *goes out the back.*

SALLY:	I'll be in the kitchen if you want me Bovey, Leigh, you're in charge out here for the moment!

SALLY *exits into the kitchen.*

The doorbell is sounded, and BYRON BAY *enters.*

BYRON:	Good day gorgeous!
LEIGH:	[*girly laugh*] Oh hello Byron. Can I get you something?
BYRON:	I just hope you know CPR, because you took my breath away!
LEIGH:	[*girly laugh*] Byron, I'm blushing!
BYRON:	No seriously, I just wanted to know if you're up for the taster session this afternoon?
LEIGH:	Sorry. [*pause*] What am I tasting?
BYRON:	No, it means a free session, to see if you like it!
LEIGH:	As we've just met, I'm not sure …
BYRON:	The surfboard session. 2 p.m.
LEIGH:	Oh yes, of course. Is it one on one?
BYRON:	What on the surfboard? Yeah, not much room for more than that!
LEIGH:	No, I meant, me as the student and you as the teacher. One on one.
BYRON:	Oh! [*pause*] No. We usually have a group of six. It's great fun and then afterwards, I'm doing a two for one on milkshakes!
LEIGH:	You're selling milkshakes?

BYRON: Yeah, they're great!

LEIGH: You do know this is a milkshake parlour. We also sell milkshakes. In fact, that is all we sell.

BYRON: I know that! Nothing wrong with a bit of healthy competition. I wouldn't mind if you started selling surf boards or any other equipment for water sports.

LEIGH: We come from Yorkshire. We don't do water sports. The closest we get is dad using the hose on us when it gets hot!

BYRON: Listen, I don't want to tread on anyone's toes. How about a voucher for a free milkshake?

LEIGH: Again! This is a milkshake parlour!

BYRON: Let's not fall out gorgeous! I would hate for that to happen. Let me make it up to you. How about dinner tonight, my treat?

LEIGH: [*softens*] Maybe. [*notices the milkshake on the counter*] Why don't you try our milkshake. It's my dad's latest creation. "As you like it".

BYRON: But you don't know how I like it!

LEIGH: That's what I said!

BYRON: What makes you think I was talking about the milk-shake?

LEIGH: [*girly laugh*] Oh Byron!

BYRON: [*sips at the drink*] This is actually quite good!

LEIGH: See!!

BYRON: Oh, hang on! Are these tinned blackberries?!

LEIGH: I think so, they're not really in season yet. So, we couldn't get fresh.

BYRON: You can if you know where to look! We don't use any tinned products when we make ours. 100% natural.

LEIGH: Well, [*takes it from him*] I wouldn't want to keep you from your surfboards. Maybe another time.

BYRON: Sorry! I didn't mean to offend you... Not the prettiest girl in Torquay.

LEIGH: Let's just say goodbye for now, just see how things work out. I'm really busy at the moment!

BYRON: You don't have any customers. [*looks around*] Oh, just that old bloke under the stairs. He looks like he's just come in to do a bit of writing. Maybe his shopping list.

LEIGH: That! Is a famous writer! Creating his new book! And my mother is creating his milkshake, which I can assure you is completely fresh and extremely delicious!

BYRON: Wow, you're even more gorgeous when you get angry!

LEIGH: Bye Byron. I have things to do! [*shuts the door behind him*]

LEIGH *exits into the kitchen.*

SALLY *appears with a magnificent milkshake, complete with a sparkler.*

BOVEY: How glorious. The sparkler is pure genius, my darling!

SALLY: I'll leave it here for you. Don't let me stop you from writing.

BOVEY: Not at all. It was just my shopping list.

SALLY: I was wondering Bovey, how long are you staying in Torquay?

BOVEY: For the whole summer, Suzanna.

SALLY: Sally.

BOVEY: I have a wonderful room at the Hamlet Inn. Why do you ask?

SALLY: Would there be any chance of you doing a book signing? I know your latest book isn't ready, but any of your previous books. I don't know if you could arrange to get some copies delivered. Obviously, you don't walk around with copies of all your books.

BOVEY: Well, funny you should say that. I think I did bring ten, [*pause*] or maybe twenty copies of all my other books.

SALLY:	Oh, well that would be amazing!
BOVEY:	I will have to check with my publicist …
SALLY:	Oh, yes of course.
BOVEY:	I'm joking my darling! It would be my honour! Obviously, we will have to talk about pay.
SALLY:	Oh, yes of course.
BOVEY:	Let's just say [*pause*] this table on a daily basis and one or two delightful milkshakes.
SALLY:	Oh, most definitely! I will get something arranged and run some dates by you!! Thank you, Bovey.
BOVEY:	Anything for my fans! I love to work here. You are usually quiet in the mornings!
SALLY:	Well, I wouldn't say that …
BOVEY:	Especially now that young Australian fellow has set up down by the harbour! Delightful name, now what was it? How strange, I'm usually good at names. Bondi was it?
SALLY:	Oh Byron. That won't affect us, it's a surf shop!
BOVEY:	Oh, as a detective novelist, I always listen intuitively to conversations and he specifically said he would be serving liquid refreshments of the milk and ice cream variety. Don't worry, your waitress gave him a short, sharp thrift. She escorted him out of the premises! Telling him to wait a while until they could meet for an evening rendezvous!
SALLY:	Oh really! If you could excuse me Bovey, I just need to talk to my waitress, I mean my daughter. I will send my husband out if you have any other requests.
BOVEY:	Of course! Happy to talk to Vincent.
SALLY	[*on exit*] It's Victor!
	The doorbell is sounded, and FLO *enters. She is followed closely by* PATRICIA TROUT.
FLO:	This is the place Pat.

PAT:	You know, I like to be called Patricia now.
FLO:	Yes, sorry. Now you've had your hair done, your nails and your feet. I thought we could stop and have a milk-shake. Live a little.
PAT:	I suppose so. I hope I don't get that brain freeze feeling!
FLO:	With that much Botox and lip stuff, I don't think you'll notice.
PAT:	Collagen!
FLO:	No need for that!
PAT:	No, that's what they put in my lips.
FLO:	They use to call it "Trout Pout". [*pause*] Oh, how funny is that, as Trout is your surname.
PAT:	I keep telling you it's Trutt!
FLO:	Oh, for god sake. Pat, you're Patty from Liverpool. Stand up and be proud!
PAT:	I know one thing, I can't stand much longer in these heels!
FLO:	If you hate your surname that much, you've got three more married names to fall back on. Why not your maiden name?
PAT:	May I remind you of my maiden name!
FLO:	Trollop is an acceptable name! Isn't there a writer called Trollop?
PAT:	I don't know of any writers!
BOVEY:	[*looks up from his pad*] Well, you certainly do now! Now don't be shy! I don't bite. I know it can be daunting, meeting me in the flesh, but just think of me as a normal man. That usually helps to get a grip of oneself. Yes, I am a renowned author, it is true! But I too, am able to talk to the simple folk of this town. Although I hear you are not locals. If I put my detective hat on, I believe ... You are from Liverpool!

PAT: Well, I'm …

BOVEY: Trying to re-invent yourself. That is absolutely under-standable. The Beatles survived it, but probably not a place to frequent on a more permanent basis.

FLO: I love my scouse roots …

BOVEY: I can also tell that you have style and flare!

PAT: Well, I …

BOVEY: Not dissimilar to a character, you probably already know, called Martha Frostrop. As you know she also strived to better herself! So, I say again. I am always happy to meet fans, but I do dine alone. I believe Sienna, the owner, is setting up a meet and greet.

FLO: For who?

BOVEY: For you!

FLO: To meet who?

BOVEY: Oh, I do enjoy your colloquial wit. Very refreshing and rural. I could sign a napkin if you so wish.

FLO: Listen! I came in here for a milkshake. I don't know who you are! So, unless you've been sent by "Tommy Knuckles" about his car. You can tell him, I didn't know the motor was his, when I borrowed it and I didn't mean to set it on fire! I always have a fag when I'm driving, it's habit and the whiskey just steadies my nerves!

BOVEY: Oh, I see we are at cross purposes. I should have realised; an admiration of literacy was not going to be the case. Not a fiction connoisseur but a mere older lady trying to survive in difficult circumstances! [*pause*] People are so extraordinary! I must write that down. [*picks up pen and pad*] Mature lady, in strife, other lady held together with cosmetic surgery and market high heels.

PAT: I beg your pardon?

BOVEY: Ladies, let us start again. I am Bovey Tracey.

FLO:	Ok.
BOVEY:	I am a writer of many successful novels! I find your incomprehension of my status rather refreshing, like my delicious milkshake. Please sit! At the next table, and let me buy you both a milkshake, as a way of smoothing things over.
FLO:	I suppose.
BOVEY:	You will inevitably realise, today's meeting, will become a wonderful memory for you. Maybe the best you will have, in the few years you have left, until you shuffle off this immortal coil.
PAT:	Writer you say? Unlike my companion. I have dabbled in a spot of writing.
FLO:	Since when?
BOVEY:	Fascinating.
PAT:	Not published! Just short stories!
BOVEY:	Fascinating. I would be happy to give you writing tips, or any advice on how to improve your work.
PAT:	That would be good!
BOVEY:	I shall give you my card!
PAT:	[*reads the card*] Bovey Tracey – "A delightful novelist, capable of mingling humour with sharp poignancy. Tracey's narration is so elegantly laced with wit". Says *The Torquay Observer* – Winner of "Torquay's writers' competition 2018 and 2019". That's a lot to put on a business card! As well as email, telephone number and address. Oh and "Facebook". Very modern.
BOVEY:	Now, you know all about me ladies, are you now ladies of leisure? In your mature years.
FLO:	Mostly.
PAT:	I don't know exactly what you mean "mature" years. I trained many years ago at Mersey University.
FLO:	She means Liverpool Tech …

PAT:	And for many years, I have run a successful chain of salons.
FLO:	Chain?
PAT:	Maybe, I should give you my card.
BOVEY:	Well, I ...
	VICTOR *appears from the kitchen*.
VICTOR:	Everything to your satisfaction, Mr Tracey?
BOVEY:	Truly wonderful, Vincent.
VICTOR:	It's Victor. [*sees FLO and PAT*] Oh ladies, welcome. So glad to see you come back with your friend!
FLO:	Deffo. This kind man has said he's going to buy us a couple of milkshakes, so, if we could see the menus.
VICTOR:	Of course. [*grabs a couple of menus*] Here you both are. May I recommend ... everything.
PAT:	I would like something refreshing and fruity!
VICTOR:	Wouldn't we all! [*laughs*]
FLO:	Cheeky!! I want something sweet and sickly, the more calorific the better. Patricia's lost six stone, so probably just a straw in a cup of air!
PAT:	Flo, don't be silly.
FLO:	Sorry, only messing!
VICTOR:	I think you, Patricia, will enjoy, "Summers day", a combination of fresh summer fruits and cream!
PAT:	Sounds very nice, thank you!
FLO:	Yeah, I prefer mine with a touch of ...
VICTOR:	Chocolate?
FLO:	No ... booze.
VICTOR:	Oh yes, of course, any particular brand.
FLO:	One with the most percentage!
VICTOR:	Well, I can recommend our Creamy Coconut Rum shake. We called it "The Hamlet Pirate".

FLO:	Oooh pirates are so sexy. I love that Johnny Depp!
VICTOR:	It is quite strong! And it is only 10.30 in the morning!
FLO:	Where I come from that's practically lunch time!
VICTOR:	Just be careful!
FLO:	Maybe even *you'll* start looking like Johnny Depp!
VICTOR:	Don't take too big a mouthful!
FLO:	That's what Johnny Depp said!
PAT:	Flo!!
FLO:	That reminds me of a joke. Where are your bucca-neers? Under your b …
PAT:	Flo!! That's enough!
VICTOR:	Ok, one "Summer's Day" and one "The Hamlet Pirate"
FLO:	Listen, no skimping on the rum!
VICTOR:	Wouldn't dream of it.
PAT:	Thank you!
FLO:	I once had a bottle of rum on me cornflakes!
VICTOR:	Wonderful! I'll be back shortly! [*exits*]
FLO:	Who's he calling shorty!
PAT:	Flo, for goodness' sake, just calm down.
FLO:	Sorry, just getting into the holiday spirit!
	Voices off, of SALLY and LEIGH.
SALLY:	[*off stage*] Don't you walk away from me young lady!
LEIGH:	[*off stage*] There is nothing left to say!
	They enter. SALLY has large bag with her.
LEIGH:	Yes, he had a milkshake, it was just a taster, and yes, the blackberries were tinned, and he did notice, but it doesn't mean anything!!!
SALLY:	You just don't need to disclose all the information.
LEIGH:	What's with the big bag?
SALLY:	Donations!

LEIGH:	For who?
SALLY:	The charity shop!
LEIGH:	Since when do you donate to charity?
SALLY:	Since always.
LEIGH:	You always say charity begins at home.
SALLY:	Oh Leigh! [*over the top laughing*] You are sooo funny!!
LEIGH:	Do you even know where the charity shops are?
SALLY:	Yes, thank you.
	[*very perky*] Good morning ladies, how are we this morning?
PAT:	Very well thank you.
SALLY:	Victor will be out shortly; they do take a bit of time on the account of the ingredients all being completely fresh! Leigh will be here if you need anything else. I hope to see you again! If not have a lovely holiday!
	She exits.
	VICTOR *comes in with the two milkshakes.*
VICTOR:	Here you are ladies! [*looks around*] Leigh, where's Sally?
LEIGH:	Mum went to the charity shop.
VICTOR:	Oh yes. She took my advice then. I told her, there's nothing wrong with charity shops. I said why spend good money on clothes when you can wear someone else's for half the price. I know, it's often people that have passed away who have donated. Well not them obviously, their family has. I mean if you needed a new lung, we'd take a second hand one that someone had donated, so why not a jumper or a cagoule!
LEIGH:	It's not quite the same!
VICTOR:	If I'd have known she was going. I could have asked her to look for some trunks for me, mine have a got a great big hole in them and believe me, it's not a pretty sight!!
LEIGH:	Dad, gross!!

VICTOR:	You could do with some clothes as well, those jeans you wear are full of holes!
LEIGH:	That's the fashion! [*pause*] Anyway she went to donate, not buy.
VICTOR:	Donate? Since when does she donate to charity?
LEIGH:	That what I said, she always says charity begins at home.
VICTOR:	Does she even know where the charity shops are?
LEIGH:	That's what I said. [*looks out the window*]
PAT:	Sorry to interrupt, but could I possibly borrow your facilities?
VICTOR:	Of course.
FLO:	Has it gone right through you Pat?
PAT:	No, I just need to powder my nose.
VICTOR:	Yes of course, through the arch, on the right!
	PAT *exits.*
FLO:	This is a lovely milkshake. I'm really enjoying it!
VICTOR:	Good, I'm glad to hear it.
FLO:	You know it really is quite strong!
VICTOR:	Yes, I did say, you should take it easy. You look like you've already finished it!
FLO:	It was just so scrummy!
VICTOR:	Maybe sit for a while. The sea air may make you a bit whoosy!
FLO:	You're lovely, you are! What's your name again?
VICTOR:	Victor.
FLO:	Victor. Like victorious! Or viscount! Wasn't there a biscuit called Viscount?
VICTOR:	I'm not sure.

FLO:	[*slurring*] Yeah, there was! It had a green wrapper, milk chocolate. It was round. I think it had mint in it. Did it have mint in it?
VICTOR:	I'm not sure.
FLO:	I'm sure it had a mint in it! Here! Boosey Tracey! Did it have mint in it?
BOVEY:	Not a chocolate biscuit I am familiar with, I'm afraid.
FLO:	Do you live around here?
BOVEY:	No, I have a flat in Chelsea. I spend the summers here. I originally come from Torquay. It's the inspiration for all my novels.
FLO:	Lovely!
BOVEY:	You can't beat an early morning walk along the cliffs or down on the beach.
FLO:	I bet! Where are you staying?
BOVEY:	At the Hamlett Inn, it's small, but quite charming.
FLO:	We're above the chippie in a B&B. It's the one called "The fry up" and the B&B upstairs, is called "The fry up-stairs" how funny is that!
BOVEY:	Yes, very amusing.
FLO:	It was Pat's idea. [*pause*] Sorry *Patricia*! I don't know why, she's not really a fan of the sea or the beach, come to think of it, she's not really a fan of anything! I love the seaside! Victor! Can I have another one love?
VICTOR:	How about a "Bean and gone"?
FLO:	What's that when it's at home?
VICTOR:	A Frappuccino.
FLO:	A frappe who?
VICTOR:	A milkshake blend with a shot of strong coffee.
FLO:	Oh, alright then! [*pause*] How long does it take her to go to the loo! Probably doing her hair in there! I'll go and check on her. The blonde's not real, you know. If you look over the lavvy door you would soon see!

FLO *exits. Almost as if the door is revolving. As soon as* FLO *leaves* PAT *returns.*

VICTOR: Leigh, would you mind holding the fort while I make Flo her milkshake?

LEIGH: Ok.

VICTOR *exits.*

PAT: Hopefully, she won't pass out on the toilet. [*looks in her bag*] Oh!!

LEIGH: Are you ok?

PAT: I seem to have misplaced my purse. Oh dear! Erm can you tell Flo when she comes back, I've just gone back to the bed and breakfast. I'll try and retrace my steps!

LEIGH: Yes of course. I'll let your friend know, my dad is making her a milkshake with a strong coffee in it.

PAT *leaves the sound of the doorbell and the door shutting.*

LEIGH: So, Mr Tracey, what novel are you working on now?

BOVEY: It's another mystery of course, my fifth in the series of "English Riviera mysteries". This one focuses in a country village. The residents are in the process of setting up the village fete. One of the most popular activities is that of the muffin competition. The locals all make their mouth-watering, original muffins to be judged for a competition.

LEIGH: Oh yes.

BOVEY: Well, the day before the prestigious event, one of the competitors is found dead!

LEIGH: Oh dear.

BOVEY: Yes! It will have you on the edge of your seat.

LEIGH: So, who is the killer?

BOVEY: You will have to read the book, young lady.

LEIGH: Yes, I suppose so.

BOVEY: Now, I have just remembered, I have to call my agent. We have to arrange my winter tour. I will leave this fine establishment, but return anon. I presume my table will be here when I get back. I will probably only be gone for a short while.

LEIGH: Yes, that will be fine.

BOVEY: Very good young lady. Here is a crisp ten-pound note, for the milkshakes purchased by the seniors. I will return shortly.

LEIGH: Alright, see you later.

BOVEY exits. The doorbell sounds and the door is shut.

A loud screech is heard from the toilet!

FLO/VOICE OFF: Help! Help! I'm stuck, I can't get out! Help, Help.

LEIGH: Oh, my goodness! Don't worry! Dad!!

VICTOR appears.

VICTOR: What's happened!?

LEIGH: It's that drunk old lady, she says she's stuck in the toilet!

VICTOR: Well, is she?

LEIGH: I don't know!

VICTOR: Well, why don't you go and check?!

FLO: [*voice off*] Help, help, I'm getting claustrophobic!

LEIGH: Alright, I'm coming.

LEIGH exits. Pause. She then returns.

LEIGH: Yes, she's definitely stuck!

VICTOR: What *in* the actual toilet?

LEIGH: No, the lock's jammed.

PAT returns.

PAT: Everything ok?

VICTOR: No! [*whispers*] Apparently Flo is stuck in our bathroom.

PAT:	Oh dear! She always manages to do that! She somehow manages to jam any lock going. The good news is because I've experienced it before. I know just how to jiggle it and get her out.
VICTOR:	If you could that would be great.
PAT:	No problem.

PAT *exits and returns with* LEIGH *and a rather scared looking* FLO.

FLO:	I saw my whole life flash before me! It's funny, I did it before in the bed and breakfast, didn't I Patricia? I don't think I know my own strength.
VICTOR:	No harm done, take a seat and I'll bring you your milkshake!
FLO:	Oh, you are kind.
PAT:	Thank you very much Victor!
FLO:	It was like that weekend I spent at my cousin's, back in the eighties.
PAT:	What, the décor or the facilities.
FLO:	No, we got locked in a phone box on Rhiland Street. [*pause*] Smelt the same as well.
PAT:	It's alright, it's over Flo.
FLO:	No, it didn't overflow. I made sure I didn't put the plug in the sink! Good job you came back Patricia.
PAT:	Always!

The doorbell sounds and BOVEY TRACEY *enters.*

BOVEY:	Wonderful news everyone! I have just secured my winter tour, extravaganza.

VICTOR *enters with the milkshake for* FLO.

VICTOR:	Here you are Flo.
FLO:	Ta! Looks stunning!
BOVEY:	Starting in picturesque Croxley Green, to the heights of rural Tring and ending up in the quaint hamlet of

Pickled Herring. A beautiful village overlooking a dazzling brook. The book signing will be in the local bakery. I hear they can sometimes accommodate ten people if the chairs are place in a certain way! Aptly named "Much Ado about muffins" which, is in fact, the title of my latest book.

LEIGH: Great news!

BOVEY: A very small venue, I am told. Quite compact, walls, not that far apart ...

FLO: Please don't talk about small spaces!!

BOVEY: Valentino! Valentino another milkshake please!

VICTOR: It's Victor. I shall go and make your order.

BOVEY: I have a good feeling about this tour!

FLO: Oh my god!!

BOVEY: No, you do not need to be concerned. I can be very creative on a book tour; I once gave a talk to the Women's institute. The setting was under a beautiful gazebo, by a Silverston stream. I was suddenly interrupted by a rather disagreeable tribe of protestors, with a rather large banner, disputing testing deodorants and soaps on animals, unfortunately that seemed to suggest they didn't believe in using any deodorants or soaps themselves.

LEIGH's *phone rings.*

LEIGH: Sorry, I won't be a second. Hello Byron. [*goes off to a quiet part of the parlour*]

BOVEY: So, I managed to avoid a scene and suggested they go into the town.

PAT: Why was that?

BOVEY: I told them there was a large cosmetic factory down by the mill.

PAT: And was there?

BOVEY: No mill or cosmetic factory. So, I cut my losses and left, just in case the angry tribe returned.

FLO: Awful!!

BOVEY: Oh, you know, I just needed to think on my feet!

FLO: No, this milkshake!

BOVEY: Oh, surely not!

FLO: There's salt in my milkshake!

LEIGH: Sorry I have to go Byron; a customer is complaining about salt in her drink.

FLO: I know I said I like the sea, but I don't want to drink it!

LEIGH: Are you sure?

FLO: I know what salt tastes like!

LEIGH: Dad could you come out here please.

VICTOR *returns with* BOVEY's *ice cream.*

VICTOR: Is there a problem?

FLO: Yes, it's salty!

VICTOR: It can't be.

FLO: Try it!

VICTOR *tries the milkshake.*

VICTOR: Oh, my goodness. I do apologise, but I can't understand it. It's my usual ice cream blend. I'll get you some water.

VICTOR *exits and returns with a glass of water.*

VICTOR: Maybe Bovey, just wait a moment until ...

BOVEY *takes a mouthful.*

BOVEY: Mine is perfectly fine. I will sit here with my notepad and enjoy this delightful creation.

VICTOR: Then it must be the coffee. Leigh would you come out the back with me please?

LEIGH: If I must.

LEIGH *exits.*

VICTOR: I am so sorry Flo. I will return as soon as I have some answers.

VICTOR *exits.*

Just then the doorbell rings and BYRON *appears.*

BYRON: G'day all and what a beautiful day it is!

PAT: Maybe we should just go Flo.

FLO: Maybe just the glass of water for now. I'm still a bit woozy and it was only one sip. Anyway, I'm enjoying the view!

BYRON: Well, hello beautiful ladies. Can I introduce myself, I'm Byron. I own the new surf shop down by the harbour. I'm doing a free taster session this afternoon.

FLO: What are we tasting?

BYRON: No, it's a surfboard lesson. Free of charge, on the understanding, I get to see your beautiful faces for a lesson later on in the week.

FLO: I never been on a surfboard before.

PAT: Oh, I don't think so …

BYRON: No, it's real fun, I promise! I would be really gentle with you.

FLO: Would you get on with me, just to show me how it's done?

BYRON: Well, no, but you can start off slow.

FLO: Start off slow …

BYRON: Yeah, you can just lie on it to start with.

FLO: Do I have to wear one of them all in one things?

BYRON: A wet suit, yeah.

FLO: Oh, no! My brother wore one once, he went in the sea and started waving his arms and legs manically. We thought he was having a funny turn. Turns out he'd got a crab caught in it! After that, he never went in the sea again. They still call him Crabby Colin!

PAT:	I don't think that's why Flo.
FLO:	Then my cousin Rita. Do you remember her Patricia?
PAT:	I think so.
FLO:	She wore one … to a hen party. Needless to say, she had too much to drink and wanted the loo. She couldn't get it undone. You know with the zip being at the back. Anyway, she panicked, asked the bar man to undo her! He got his button stuck in the zip and she ended up carrying him on her back.
BYRON:	And?
FLO:	So, then the bouncer thought it was a pub fight, and ripped them apart! Which also ripped the wetsuit, straight down the middle. The top half completely in shreds!
BYRON:	So, setting her free!
FLO:	Yeah, top half completely wetsuit free!
BYRON:	Fantastic!
FLO:	Until she realised, she wasn't wearing anything underneath.
BYRON:	Oh, embarrassing!
FLO:	She wasn't really worried about that, most of the lads in the pub had seen them.
BYRON:	So …
FLO:	Well, she'd just got engaged to Jimmy.
BYRON:	Yes?
FLO:	But she was also seeing Cliff.
BYRON:	And?
FLO:	Well, the night before, they'd gone out and she'd had a tattoo done with the name Cliff. Jimmy was there, as it was the local pub and went mental. Rita tried to make out it was because she liked cliffs in general. You know, like white cliffs of Dover. But Jimmy wasn't buying it! Disaster!

BYRON:	Wow, that's quite a story.
PAT:	Isn't it?!
BYRON:	And you, Patricia?
PAT:	Oh, no, no horror stories about wetsuits.
BYRON:	Fancy a session?
PAT:	I think not!
FLO:	She doesn't like to get her hair wet. Mind you, you could show off your new figure Patricia. She's lost five stone you know!
BYRON:	Wow, that's incredible!
FLO:	Re-invented herself she has!
PAT:	Yes, thank you, Flo. I'm afraid. I won't be joining you though. A walk by the beach might do us good though, Flo.
FLO:	Maybe in a bit. So, Byron, what's a nice young man like you doing in a place …
	LEIGH *returns*.
LEIGH:	Erm, yes it was the coffee, I am so sorry Flo. Oh Byron, I didn't know you were here.
BYRON:	Well, I …
	VICTOR *enters*.
VICTOR:	I'm afraid everyone there's a flood in the kitchen. The freezer isn't working, and the ice cream has gone like liquid.
LEIGH:	So, now the freezer isn't working, what's going on!?
VICTOR:	It's worse than that.
LEIGH:	How can it be worse than that?
VICTOR:	Someone has unplugged it.
	Just then the doorbell rings and SALLY *appears, still carrying her large bag.*
LEIGH:	I need to sit down!

SALLY: Vic, I need to talk to you!

VICTOR: In a minute love, why have you still got that bag with you?

SALLY: Oh, this, the erm shop was shut. I need to talk to you.

VICTOR: I need to talk to you; it seems someone has a problem with us.

SALLY: I know!

VICTOR: And we need to … What do you mean you know!?

SALLY: I couldn't believe it when I saw it!

VICTOR: Me neither. It's all ruined!

SALLY: Well, I don't think it's that bad!

VICTOR: But it's all over the floor.

SALLY: What is?

VICTOR: The ice cream!

SALLY: The what?

VICTOR: Ice cream! Cold stuff. Comes in different flavours.

SALLY: Yes, I know what ice cream is. Why is it on the floor!?

VICTOR: Someone unplugged our freezer!

SALLY: Oh, my goodness!

VICTOR: So, what were you talking about!

SALLY: We have a review on our website!

VICTOR: Well, that's ok.

SALLY: This one isn't, it's terrible. Oh, this is a disaster!

VICTOR: So, someone is deliberately trying to sabotage the business!

BYRON: It looks like you have stuff to deal with, I'll come back later.

VICTOR: You!!

Scene 2

BOVEY: Nobody move! Vernon lock the door!!

VICTOR: It's Victor!

SALLY: You, Bovey? Did you write the bad review ...?

BOVEY: Absolutely not! Please Sharon, let me see the review.

SALLY: It's Sally.

BOVEY: [*reading*] When you think of the picturesque village of Torquay, you imagine a milkshake parlour to fit its postcard seenery. "Shakes Here" milkshakes are not as pretty as a picture. I went there hoping to have one of their impressive looking shakes only to recieve a drink with salt in it! Also, I was informed that the blackberries were out of a tin! I'm not usually one to give bad reviews but I wanted to save people the journey.

VICTOR: You like to write, Bovey. How do we know it's not you?

BOVEY: Yes, *write* being the operative word and I have the ability to spell! 'Receive' is spelt incorrectly and so is 'scenery'! Also, anyone with half a brain would know, Torquay is a town and not a village.

VICTOR: Unless they didn't really know about *English* places at all! A foreigner, perhaps ...

BYRON: Hey, wait a minute!

BOVEY: So, let's just look at what we know. Everyone here has been a visitor this morning to this establishment and may have experienced or overheard, the talk of tinned fruit and salt!

FLO: Well, I had the salt, but I don't have a phone! I don't like to be tracked!

BOVEY: So, as an expert in mystery novels, I think we can all agree, that it is possibly someone in this room. Obviously, I don't want to accuse anyone, and you are all free to leave. Although that may make you look, somewhat guilty.

BYRON: I'm staying here! Until my name is cleared!

BOVEY: So, we need to think of the evidence and the motive!

FLO: But you went out Mr Tracey. It could have been you!

BOVEY: Yes, it could have been. How are you to believe that I phoned my agent? Here is my phone. Shall we call it Exhibit A?

Laura, will you look at the phone and find the dialled calls?

LEIGH: It's Leigh.

BOVEY: Yes.

LEIGH: Ok, it says today. Mum and Farrington Turner.

BOVEY: Well, yes. I phone my mother. She is 89 and lives alone. And Farrington is my agent.

LEIGH: Could be code!

BOVEY: You may dial them young lady and put it on speaker.

She dials. A ringing tone is heard.

Voice of old lady is heard.

VIOLET: Malcolm, can I phone you back love. I'm just eating my steak and kidney pudding and if I rush it, I get indigestion. Do you mind? It's just the right temperature. Is it urgent? We did speak earlier, is it still your trapped wind?

BOVEY: It's fine, Mum!

BOVEY *hurriedly takes the phone and cuts it off.*

LEIGH: Shall I try the other number, Malcolm?

BOVEY: If you would!

She dials. A ringing tone is heard.

Voice business-like voice is heard.

FARRINGTON: Bovey, I thought we just cleared this up! I know your last book wasn't as successful as you hoped, but I really think the kids' books will work out fine. Yes, it's a one-eyed donkey, but it will be fun! Just think of ... A Pirate Eeyore!

BOVEY: Of course, sorry Farrington, I'm losing signal. [*pause as* BOVEY *terminates the call*] I hope that has cleared up any misunderstandings or accusations.

LEIGH: I had another idea! Newton Abbot!!

VICTOR: Yes. Newton Abbot, the owner of the property.

LEIGH: I thought I could look up his Facebook page, but it just comes up as the place!

VICTOR: Try Christopher Bacon. That's his real name.

FLO: Looks like everyone likes to be named after places! Here, Patricia maybe you should be "Ivy Bridge" and I "Teignmouth".

PAT: More like loudmouth!

LEIGH: Oh, here he is. [*pause*] Oh, there's a photo of him, he's at "The Rocky Horror" sing along cinema screening down in Cornwall. Just let me have a look at something. Yes, it was this morning. The cinema is in the background, so he's definitely too far away to have un-plugged the freezer.

BOVEY: So, I am in the clear and so it the owner. I doubt Vernon or Louise would sabotage their own business, although Stephanie ...

SALLY: Sally.

BOVEY: You were gone for quite some time.

SALLY: Well, yes, but it's my business as well.

BOVEY: A trip to the charity shop you say to take some donations. But we all see you have brought the same bag back.

SALLY:	Well, I refilled it with purchases from the charity shop.
BOVEY:	You said it was closed.
SALLY:	It was, so I went to another.
BOVEY:	I see, what was this shop called?
SALLY:	Err, it was the "Tortoise appreciation society" charity shop.
BOVEY:	Most unusual.
SALLY:	Alright, you've got me. I didn't go to the charity shop. [*pause*] I went for a swim; this is my swimming bag. Look! [*removes a costume and towel*]
LEIGH:	That's my costume!
SALLY:	Sorry, I was in a hurry!
BOVEY:	So, yes that leaves us with our two senior ladies and Byron! Byron certainly has the motive. A rival business, also selling milkshakes.
BYRON:	But I didn't have a milkshake with salt in it!
LEIGH:	No, but I did tell you on the phone and you mentioned the tinned blackberries!
BYRON:	Yes, but Leigh. I told you! I'm not out to ruin your family's business! I wouldn't. I'm not even interested in the milkshake side of things. I'll stick to surfing! It wasn't me!
BOVEY:	But no one else has a motive! You came in earlier, you left and only reappeared after all the unfortunate events had occurred!
BYRON:	I promise you, it wasn't me!
SALLY:	It wasn't Byron!
VICTOR:	How do you know?
SALLY:	Because he was with me!
VICTOR:	He was, was he?!
SALLY:	Not like that. He was teaching me how to surf. It was a big group of us. He was teaching us the whole time.

LEIGH:	That explains why you wore my costume. Uggh Mum!
BYRON:	You can see my signing in sheet. I have contacts for all the students for the morning!
BOVEY:	That won't be necessary.
BYRON:	But you were convinced it was me!
BOVEY:	Initially, when you just walked in, but then … I had another hunch, and suddenly all the pieces just fitted together. Someone else was out for revenge. I remember Vincent mentioning he went to Liverpool Tech, and so did you Patricia.
PAT:	So, what? How is that a motive?! I obviously went way before Victor did.
BOVEY:	You would think so, yes, but Leigh maybe you should have checked my browser history. Liverpool Tech was only a tech for a year. Before that it was a college and then it became a university. So yes, you would have been there as a mature student.
	Flo has been invaluable with her loose lips, telling us how Patricia had lost a lot of weight and the facelifts. No doubt a few hair colour changes too. A phoney accent and a change of name would make her almost unrecognisable.
FLO:	Trollop!
PAT:	I beg your pardon!
FLO:	That was her name, Patsy Trollop.
BOVEY:	And just to put in my final piece of evidence, a small white salt packet. Stuck to the bottom of my milkshake glass! At first, I thought just a torn serviette, but not a salt packet [*produces It*] A piece of evidence; I have securely stowed away. It's the type of branded salt packet you get in a particular type of establishment. Leigh, would you like to read what it says on it?
LEIGH:	"The fry up" …
FLO:	Pat! You could have killed me!

PAT:	That wasn't my intention. But knowing your big mouth, I should have used arsenic, or at least left you locked in the toilet!
FLO:	That was you as well!?
PAT:	Yes, I needed a distraction. I needed to write the review … The spelling errors must have been that silly auto predict button. I then had to walk around the back of the parlour to add the salt and unplug the freezer. I needed everyone to be focusing on something else and somewhere else!
FLO:	Patsy, how could you?
VICTOR:	Patsy Trollop! Of course! Now I remember. You were the teacher's star pupil, until I came along. She said my crème brûlée was to die for! The perfect layer of hardened caramelized sugar. Like a perfect frozen lake! She said it was restaurant quality!
PAT:	Exactly, it was tiresome! So, when it came to the final exam. I panicked, and the more I panicked the more I added the wrong ingredients. Rubbery prawns, a tablespoon of horseradish – not a teaspoon. Too much ginger. It was a total flop!! And as usual, your souffle was to die for. Like a perfect Mount Fuji!
FLO:	For goodness' sake! What is this? Disaster chef!!
VICTOR:	But this was all in the past.
FLO:	Move on!
PAT:	All my dreams shattered. I had to take an evening class in hairdressing! I couldn't face cooking anymore and that was the only class that had spaces!
VICTOR:	So, it was fate! But now you have a successful business! You said so yourself.
PAT:	Hardly. I didn't sign a prenup – and husband number two, took it from me! I have nothing. I'm even living back with my sister.
FLO:	I didn't know that.

PAT:	So, no home, no business. I'm just a worker and a [*scouse accent returns*] dosser, on someone's sofa! I don't own anything. And then ...
FLO:	What?
PAT:	Facebook.
FLO:	Facebook?
PAT:	Yes, when we met for coffee.
FLO:	Oh, I knew it was going to be my fault again. I told you I visited that bondage page by mistake.
PAT:	Not that page!
FLO:	I thought that other page was well known piano play-ers. I didn't realise it said "Big peni ...
PAT:	Not that one either!
FLO:	Made me eyes water!
PAT:	The other page ...
FLO:	Oh, was it when I went on the Torquay visitors page?
PAT:	Yes, and who should pop up, all smug? One Victor Abbey, flourishing business, and beautiful family. Sickening!
BOVEY:	The green-eyed monster reared its ugly head!
FLO:	Yeah, she's not a pleasant sight in the morning!
VICTOR:	I'm sorry you feel like that, Patsy. I didn't set out to hurt you!
PAT:	I know! They say revenge is sweet, but it isn't. I feel even worse now that I tried to sabotage your business ... I'll pay for any damages. I'm sorry.
FLO:	He might want to call the police!
PAT:	Yes, thank you Flo.
VICTOR:	No, I won't, but I do know something that could make this right!
PAT:	What are you thinking?

VICTOR: Well, this property has an extra two rooms upstairs. Never been used.

PAT: And?

VICTOR: Large space, a few chairs. Ladies facials, nails ... the other room's big enough for a bed, there's a sink and toilet!

PAT: Really?

VICTOR: Yeah, to be honest. We're struggling with the rent, and in the winter, we leave this place empty. We always said it would be good to have someone in, to keep an eye on the place. Obviously once you get on your feet, we'll make a proper agreement. Share bills and rent. What do you think?

PAT: I feel worse now!

VICTOR: Why?

PAT: Because yet again, you've shown how nice you are!

VICTOR: What do you say?

PAT: It sounds fantastic! Victor?

VICTOR: Yes?

PAT: Thank you.

VICTOR: Just to prove I'm not that nice. How about dinner at "The fry up"!! On you of course!

PAT: Definitely! All of you must come.

PAT *opens the door and heads out. In couples, they leave the milkshake parlour.*

BYRON: So, now my good name has been cleared, can I sit next to you, gorgeous?

LEIGH: Yes, I suppose so.

BYRON *and* LEIGH *exit.*

SALLY: Oh, yes, I fancy a battered sausage. I like a large one!

VICTOR: I know!

SALLY: Ooh, cheeky!

VICTOR *and* SALLY *exit.*

BOVEY: My dear? [*offers his arm for* FLO *to take*]

FLO: What a gentleman! Do you like the chippie?

BOVEY: I think it is an acquired taste. Let's just say, I prefer a good book, a merlot, and some Pavarotti!

FLO: Oh yeah, I love that with extra cream, although sometimes the meringue gets stuck in me teeth!

They exit.

www.ingramcontent.com/pod-product-compliance
Lightning Source LLC
Chambersburg PA
CBHW050907180626
46814CB00007B/2932